The Usborne
Little Book
of
Birds

First published in 2008 by Usborne Publishing Ltd.,
Usborne House, 83-85 Saffron Hill, London, EC1N 8RT, England
www.usborne.com

Printed in Dubai

The Usborne
Little Book
of
Birds

Sarah Khan

Designed by Kate Rimmer,
Nayera Everall and Michael Hill

Digital manipulation by Keith Furnival

Consultant: Derek Niemann
Youth Editor for the Royal Society
for the Protection of Birds

Edited by Kirsteen Rogers

Internet links

There are lots of fun websites where you can find out more about birds. We have created links to some of the best sites on the Usborne Quicklinks Website. To visit the sites, go to www.usborne-quicklinks.com and type in the keywords "little birds". Here are some of the things you can do on the internet:

🖋 Take a virtual flight with a golden eagle
🖋 Watch videos and listen to sound clips of a huge array of birds
🖋 Create your own birds and see how they would survive in different environments

Bird pictures to download

You can download many of the pictures in this book from the Usborne Quicklinks Website. These pictures are for personal use only and must not be used for commercial purposes.

Internet safety

The websites recommended in Usborne Quicklinks are regularly reviewed. However, the content of a website may change at any time and Usborne Publishing is not responsible for the content of websites other than its own. We recommend that children are supervised while on the internet.

Contents

About birds

Soaring through the air, singing in treetops or gliding through water, birds can be seen almost everywhere. There are 10,000 kinds and probably more yet to be discovered.

What makes a bird a bird?

Even the tiniest hummingbird and the tallest ostrich have features in common. Like all birds, they have one beak, two legs and wings, and hundreds of feathers. They also hatch from eggs and can keep their bodies at a constant temperature.

Colourful Eurasian nuthatches are stout birds with thick legs and feet.

Europe's smallest bird, goldcrests are quiet and unassuming, with thin legs and dull feathers, apart from a yellow head stripe.

American northern cardinals are loud and flashy, with a distinctive crest of feathers on the top of their heads.

Early birds

Scientists think that the first birds appeared 145 million years ago, at the time of the dinosaurs. As well as having feathers and wings like modern birds, these prehistoric creatures also possessed sharp teeth and long, bony tails.

Today's birds are descended from feathered prehistoric creatures, such as this Archaeopteryx.

Where birds live

Birds are skilled survivors that have adapted to live in all types of environments – from lush tropical rainforests to freezing polar ice caps. The varied landscapes of Europe are home to over 500 species of bird.

Magpies fly from tree to tree in parks and gardens.

Puffins nest on towering cliffs.

Blackbirds sing from branches on farmland and in woods.

Mallards splash about in ponds and lakes.

Changing places

The particular surroundings a bird lives in, such as farmland or marshes, are called its habitat. As the seasons change, some birds change habitats. Others always choose the same kind of habitat, even if they spend different seasons in different countries.

This exotic-looking grassland bird is a hoopoe. Like many hoopoes, it divides its time between the open, grassy plains of Africa and the green fields of Europe.

Top to toe

Although birds all have the same basic shape and body parts, the closer you look, the more fascinating variations you'll soon spot.

Winging it

Whether a bird mainly flits, swoops or soars depends on its wing design. Even the movement of some flightless birds, such as penguins, can be affected by the shape and size of their wings.

Curved, pointed wings help swallows speed like arrows through the air.

Eagles keep their broad wings stretched out to glide on the breeze.

Legs and feet

When on land and in the water, birds rely on their legs and feet, not only to keep them moving, but often also to keep them safe and fed. The length and form of their limbs are suited to the jobs they need to do.

Strong, muscly feet help ptarmigans scratch in the ice and snow to uncover seeds and insects.

Sedge warblers have flexible toes, with one pointing backwards, which is ideal for grasping perches.

Long legs help wading birds, like this stilt, to keep their feathers dry while searching for food in deep water.

Balancing acts

A bird's tail helps it to stay balanced when on its feet, and whilst in the air, too. In flight, a bird also "steers" with its tail, adjusting the angle of it to change direction.

Long-tailed tits tilt their tails as they flit from tree to tree.

As they climb, woodpeckers hold their strong, stiff tails against a tree trunk for stability.

A wagtail's long tail helps it make sharp turns as it chases agile insects across the sky.

Beaks and bills

Birds' beaks take the place of a whole drawerful of kitchen utensils, handling food in various ways. Depending on their shape, beaks can be used for picking food up, cracking it open, sieving it from the water or ripping it apart.

A finch's cone-shaped beak is ideal for cracking open seeds.

Hooked beaks help kestrels to kill and tear up their prey.

Equipped with its long, jabbing beak, this black-tailed godwit can probe the muddy shore for insects and snails.

Dabbling ducks use their flat beaks to filter food from the water.

Fluff and feathers

Birds are the only animals with feathers. It's vital for a bird to take good care of them, as its feathery coat not only helps it to fly, but also protects it from the cold and rain.

Looking at feathers

Feathers are made of keratin, the same tough substance that makes up people's hair and nails. Every feather has a central tube-like shaft, with a flexible, soft part on either side, called a vane.

Goldfinch feather

Vane

Shaft

Close-up

Shaft

Types of feathers

A bird has three types of feathers. A layer of fluffy down feathers next to its skin helps keep it warm. These are covered by sleek body feathers, which protect it from rain and wind. Stiff flight feathers on its wings and tail push down on the air to help it fly

Down feather

Adult goose

Body feathers

Body feather

Flight feathers

Flight feather

As with all chicks, this baby goose's downy coat will be replaced with body feathers as it grows. It will still have a downy undercoat as an adult.

Taking a bath

Like people, birds bathe in water to keep clean; unlike people, many also take dust baths. They roll around on dry ground to remove lice and excess oil from their feathers. Some birds even rub ants onto their feathers, covering themselves in a lice-killing acid that the ants release from their bodies.

You might spot a bathing bird tumbling about on the dry earth...

...or making a splash in a puddle or stream.

Feather care

Birds comb their feathers with their beaks or feet. Most cover them with an oil squeezed from above their tails. This slippery goo makes their feathers waterproof and flexible, and also kills harmful germs.

Herons have a jagged edge on one of their claws, which they use like a comb to groom their feathers.

Dropping off

Birds moult regularly, shedding and replacing their damaged or worn feathers. The feathers don't drop off all at once, but over a few weeks or months. Different birds moult at different times of the year.

In summer, dunlins' feathers are brown and black.

In winter, the summer plumage is replaced by white and grey feathers.

Flying machines

When a bird flies, different parts of its body work together to keep it in the air. On the outside, its wings flap up and down, twisting to and fro, but there's lots going on inside, too.

Bones and muscles

To lift off the ground, birds must be strong, but light, too. Powerful chest muscles help them to beat their wings quickly, and hollow bones keep their bodies light. The bones are strengthened by a honeycomb-like mesh of thinner bone that supports them from the inside.

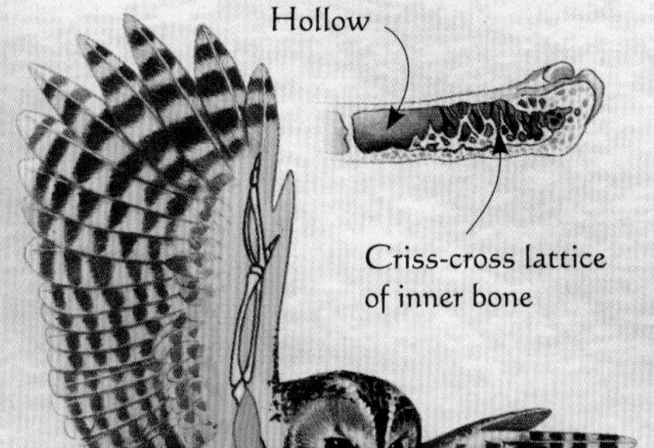

Hollow

Criss-cross lattice of inner bone

Wing bones

Beneath the feathers and skin, a bird's wing has an elbow, wrist and fingers, similar to a person's arm and hand. These bones help birds to use their wings in different ways.

A peregrine falcon glides with its wings stretched out.

A swallow folds its wings back to swoop through the air.

This diagram shows the large chest muscles that power an owl's wings.

As it hovers in search of prey, a kestrel holds its wings up.

Eye protection

As the air whistles past a flying bird, its eyes come under attack from dust, grit and drying winds. To protect them, birds have an extra, see-through eyelid, which they keep shut in flight.

The difference in air pressure above and below this Arctic tern's wings helps it rise into the air.

How wings work

In flight, streams of air flow above and below a bird's wings. The front edge of each wing is curved on top, so the air above has to flow over this curve. For the two streams to meet at the back of the wing at the same time, the stream above has to flow faster than the one below. The faster moving stream presses down less than the lower one, which helps lift the bird up.

Curved path of an air stream over a gull's wing

Power generators

Birds need a lot of energy to fly. Their hearts beat dozens of times quicker than people's hearts, to pump plenty of energy-releasing oxygen around their bodies. Smaller birds are often more active than larger ones, so their hearts beat faster still.

A chaffinch's heart can beat 1,000 times a minute.

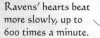

Ravens' hearts beat more slowly, up to 600 times a minute.

Birds in flight

For birds, flying is a matter of co-ordination. Whether they're taking off, landing or simply fluttering about, birds need strength, precision and perfect timing.

Getting off the ground

To many birds, taking flight means leaping up and flapping their wings as fast as they can. But some birds are too heavy for these acrobatic starts. They have to run along, flapping all the while, until they're able to rise into the air.

This big whooper swan needs a long, flappy run across the water before take-off.

Figure of eight

Up and down wingbeats lift a bird up. Once it's airborne, though, moving forwards means changing the shape of its wingbeats to a figure of eight pattern.

House sparrows flap their wings more than 12 times a second in fast flight.

The bird pushes its wings down and forwards.

As it sweeps its wings up, it opens its feathers to let air through.

When its wings are fully raised, the bird closes its feathers.

It then beats down with its wings once again.

Flight patterns

Birds don't always take the straightest path through the air. Next time you watch a bird in flight, try to imagine what pattern its path would make across the skies.

A buzzard holds out its wings to soar in a spiral on rising currents of warm air.

By flapping, then gliding on the air currents, a finch gently bounces along.

Skydivers

Some birds that hunt animals dive down from the sky to take their prey by surprise. They fold their wings back to dive, shaping their bodies like a streamlined arrow.

A goose flies fast and straight across the sky.

You might spot a streak of blue as a kingfisher dives into a river...

...or see a gannet plummeting unstoppably into the sea.

Wings lifted

Tail spread out

Coming in to land

Landing is a tricky manoeuvre. To land neatly where it wants to, a bird slows its wing beats and brings its feet forwards. Then, it lifts its wings and fans out its tail to catch the air, which slows it down enough to land safely.

Feet brought forwards

This starling is in position for an accurate landing.

On land and water

Few birds spend all their time in the air, so they have to be able to move around on land and, in some cases, through water too.

Looking at legs

At first glance, it looks as though birds' knees bend the opposite way to people's. In fact, the bends you can see are ankles. Their knees are higher up, usually hidden by feathers. Beneath the ankles are the feet, then the part that birds walk on – their toes.

To perch, this willow warbler bends its ankles, and its toes automatically curl around and lock to grip the twig.

Close-up

Ankle

Foot

Toes

Step by step

On the ground, birds move mainly by hopping with both feet together or by walking, putting one foot out at a time. There's no hard and fast rule about which birds move in which way.

As you can see here, a pheasant struts, placing one foot directly in front of the other.

Although it can break out into a run, a blackbird usually hops with both feet together.

A pigeon strides along, moving its feet forwards alternately, like a person walking.

Creepers and climbers

Climbing birds, such as woodpeckers, hop or creep up tree trunks, gobbling up insects. Most birds have one toe pointing back and three pointing forward on each foot, but woodpeckers have two toes pointing in each direction. This helps them cling steadily onto the trunks.

A green woodpecker's toes can grip even the smoothest of trunks.

Walkers and waders

Birds that spend a lot of time on the ground tend to have long, splayed-out toes to help them balance. This also spreads their weight over the surface, so that they don't sink into soft ground.

A meadow pipit's long toes let it walk around on mushy ground without sinking.

Swimmers

Most water birds have flaps of skin, called webs, between their toes. As a bird swims, it kicks its feet and stretches out its toes, using the webs as paddles to propel itself forwards. When it brings its feet back, it closes its toes, so the webs don't drag through the water.

A shoveler's footprint shows full webbing.

The webs on a shoveler's feet completely fuse its toes together, giving it maximum paddling power.

A coot's footprint shows partial webbing.

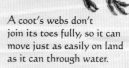

A coot's webs don't join its toes fully, so it can move just as easily on land as it can through water.

Finding food

Birds are very active and require plenty of energy. Needing food to fuel their busy lifestyles, they spend much of their time looking for their next meal.

What's for dinner?

Birds eat an amazing variety of foods. Some feed on pollen, nuts and seeds, while others prefer insects, fish or small mammals. A few even eat other birds. To drink, birds sip water, or nectar from flowers.

Swifts hunt down insects as they fly through the air.

Fieldfares eat berries, especially in the winter months.

You might spot birds like this mallard taking a mouthful of water from a pond.

A fat worm makes a delicious meal for a hungry robin.

Avoiding competition

The shape of a bird's beak helps it get to the type of food it needs. All three seed-eaters shown on the right have strong beaks to crack open the shells of seeds and nuts. But variations in their beak design help them reach different kinds of seeds, so they don't compete for one food source.

Big, sturdy beaks help hawfinches crack olive and cherry stones.

Goldfinches find seeds by poking their fine, pointed beaks into thistles and teasels.

The overlapping tips of a crossbill's beak help it split a fir cone's scales and collect the seeds inside.

Smashing shells

Some birds feast on small shelled animals, such as snails and seaside creatures. To break open their body armour, gulls and song thrushes dash the creatures against hard rocks, over and over until their shells crack.

On rocky beaches, you might see gulls bashing shells against the stones.

Now this song thrush has found a good spot for shell smashing, it will return to the same place time and again.

Food crushers

Birds don't have teeth, so they can't chew their food, and instead, swallow it in chunks. These pass into a muscly pouch near the stomach, which squeezes and squashes them to a digestible mush. Some birds gobble up small stones which stay in the pouch and help grind up really tough pieces of food.

As turnstones look for food under rocks, they swallow a few pebbles to help their digestion.

Birds of prey

Birds of prey are meat-eaters that hunt live prey or scavenge from dead animals. Of all the birds, they're among the fastest fliers, with the sharpest senses and the sharpest claws.

Air attack

To catch their prey, some hunting birds dive down from the sky, spearing their victims with their deadly talons. They then use their strong, curved beaks to pick the flesh off their lifeless victim.

A diving peregrine falcon can reach speeds of up to 180kph (112mph) – that's almost as fast as a racing car.

This kestrel is flying across the sky but, when looking for prey, it stays still, hovering in the air.

From a distance

Flying high up in the air, most birds would have trouble spotting small animals scuttling about on the ground. But birds of prey have excellent vision – around eight times sharper than a person's – so can spot their prey from far away.

A buzzard can spot a rabbit on the ground from ½km (¼mile) away.

Going fishing

Ospreys hunt fish. When they spot one, they swoop down through the air, plunge their feet into the water and seize their prey. Fish are slippery, especially when they're struggling, but an osprey has stiff spines on its feet that it can dig in to make escape impossible.

An osprey hovers above the water, waiting to see a fish near the surface.

It grabs a fish, locking its feet around its wriggling body.

Silent killers

Many owls sweep down on their unsuspecting victims in silence. Their flight feathers have fluffy, fringed edges, which muffle their wingbeats.

The soft fringes of this tawny owl's feathers reduce noise as it flies.

Night hunters

Birds that hunt at night have sharp hearing and eyesight to help them detect their prey in the gloom. Owls have big ears that hear the slightest movements, and large eyes that let in as much light as possible.

Feathers form a disc on the front of the face to funnel sounds into the ears.

Eyes at the front of the head, to help in judging distances

Ear hidden under feathers

Hide and seek

Birds come in all colours and patterns. Whether they are bright or plain often depends on whether they need to blend in with the background or stand out from the crowd.

Blending in

In the nesting season, most females stay in one spot, sitting on their eggs to keep them warm. This makes them vulnerable to attack by predators such as foxes, cats, people, and even other birds. Many mother birds are coloured in a way that matches their surroundings.

The patchy markings on a ringed plover help to camouflage it against the pebbly beaches where it nests.

When a snipe senses a predator nearby...

...it puts its head down and tail up so its stripes blend in with the grass.

It's difficult for an enemy to spot this eagle owl against the leafy ground on which it's resting.

To avoid detection, ptarmigans alter their colour with the changing seasons.

Winter plumage

Summer feathers

Hidden in the sky

Have you ever noticed how many seabirds have white bellies? As they fly above the waves looking for food, the fish can't see them against the bright sky, so the birds can swoop down and take them by surprise.

Camouflaged against the sky, these herring gulls soar above the seas and oceans, on the look-out for fish.

Identifying marks

Markings and colour can help a group of birds to stay together. Some geese, for example, use their distinctive markings to stay in sight of each other when they're flying in flocks over long distances.

Guided by the black and white rump of the bird in front, greylag geese follow the leader across the sky.

Look at me

To help them attract a mate, a male's feathers are often brighter than a female's. Some have eye-catching colours all year round, and others only develop fancy plumage when it's time to breed.

In the breeding season, a male ruff grows feathery tufts around its head and neck. Later, the tufts fall out, and plain feathers grow back.

A female common pheasant's feathers are dull.

Male common pheasants have red patches around their eyes all year round.

Male ruff in breeding season

Male after breeding season

You can tell whether a bullfinch is male or female by looking at the colour of its body.

Male

Female

Song and dance

Like people, birds have their own languages to communicate with each other. They use unique combinations of sounds and body language to get their message across.

Love songs

Birds sing most often when they're trying to find a mate. It's usually the males that perform, wooing females with ballads that can carry over long distances.

Cuckoos are named after their falling two-note song.

Nightingale songs are a melodious mix of trills, whistles and gurgles.

Male pigeons bow and coo loudly to court females.

Keep out

Love songs not only attract females, but also warn other males to stay away. If this doesn't work, and the rivals come face to face, a bird might perform a threatening display in an attempt to scare its enemy away.

Male European robins puff out their red breasts to threaten their rivals.

Copy-cat calls

Birds call out to give warnings, or to find each other. As chicks, some learn how to call by copying the sounds their parents make. Some birds can even mimic other animals, and machines.

Starlings can imitate anything from bleating sheep to ringing telephones.

Showing off

Many male birds show off to females by fluffing up their feathers, fanning out their tails, or stamping their feet in elaborate dances. In some species, the female joins in the dance, too.

Male and female grebes dance together by waggling their heads at each other...

...pulling up weeds...

...then, offering them to each other as tokens of commitment.

Putting on an act

As well as singing and dancing, some birds can act, too. Pretending to be injured, they limp along to lead predators away from their nests. Once at a safe distance, the "invalid" miraculously recovers and flies away.

A little ringed plover holds out its "broken" wing to attract a predator's attention.

Nest-builders

Once they've found a mate, most birds start making nests for the female to lay eggs inside. Many build from scratch, using materials they find lying around.

Building supplies

In spring, you'll often see busy birds flying to and fro collecting bits of twig or grass. You can help them by hanging up scraps of wool, dog hair or straw from a tree for them to use.

A few beakfuls of fluffy animal ha[ir] will help th[e] blue tit t[o] line its nest.

Rooks break off large twigs to make their nests.

A safe haven

Birds build nests anywhere that's safe from predators, often choosing places that are high above the ground or inside some kind of shelter. In winter, you can look in bare trees for nests tha[t] were used the previous summer.

Razorbills lay their eggs and raise their chicks on cliff ledges.

Sand martins dig out holes in sand banks to nest in.

Nest construction

Although birds' nests come in different shapes and sizes, most are circular. Birds weave the building materials together, constructing first the base, then the walls. As a finishing touch, they might line the nest with soft feathers or springy moss.

Long-tailed tits' nests are hollow balls made from lichens, moss, spiders' webs and feathers.

The feathers in this swallow's nest are keeping its eggs warm.

Using the grasses that grow by the water, coots weave their bowl-shaped nests on the edges of riverbanks.

Space invaders

Cuckoos don't bother to build nests of their own, but lay their eggs in other birds' nests. When the baby cuckoo hatches, it shoves the other eggs and young out of the nest, so its foster parents can fully devote themselves to raising the intruder.

A female cuckoo removes an egg from a reed warbler's nest and lays its own egg in its place.

The newly hatched cuckoo heaves out the other eggs.

The unsuspecting reed warbler parent works hard to feed the enormous cuckoo chick.

Eggs

An egg provides food and security for the baby bird forming inside it. Its structure, shape and even its colour are all designed to keep the developing chick safe.

Inside an egg

Within an egg's hard shell, floats the baby bird, cushioned by egg white and yolk. The white and yolk are food and water for the chick, and contain everything it needs to grow strong enough eventually to break out.

Egg white

Shell

Chick grows here.

Yolk

Inside its egg, this baby bird is almost ready to hatch.

Egg identification

The shell not only protects the growing chick but often makes it recognizable, too. The colours and markings on some eggshells help parent birds to identify their eggs.

Guillemots nest in large groups. They lay eggs in a vast array of shades and patterns, so parents can tell which are theirs.

Blending in

The colour of some birds' eggs helps them to blend into their surroundings hiding them from predators. Some sea birds lay their eggs in dips on pebbly beaches. The eggs' stony hues and blotchy patterns make them difficult for enemies to spot.

The markings of this little tern's egg help to camouflage it on the shingly shore.

Egg-shaped

Most eggs are oval, and are narrower at one end than the other. If knocked, an oval egg spins in a tight circle instead of rolling away from its mother or out of the nest. Birds that lay directly onto cliff ledges tend to have longer and narrower eggs, so they don't roll down the perilous slopes.

Song thrush egg

Spotted flycatcher eggs

Little owl egg

Razorbills' eggs are laid on cliffsides, so are more pointed than the others shown here.

Sitting tight

Before their eggs are laid, some parent birds shed feathers from their bellies. After laying, they sit with the bare skin, called a brood patch, covering the eggs, to keep them warm.

This marsh tit keeps all its eggs cosy with one brood patch, but some birds have many patches – one for each egg.

This kittiwake is turning round to get comfortable in its nest, as it has to sit in the same spot for long periods of time until its chick hatches out.

Growing up

A chick emerges from its shell tired, hungry and often helpless. Over the next few weeks, it must gain the strength and skill it needs to face the world alone.

Breaking free

When it's time for a chick to hatch out, it begins chipping away at the inside of its shell using a tiny bump, called an egg tooth, on the tip of its beak. While the chick is busy tapping, it calls out to let its parents know that it's on its way.

The chick uses its egg tooth to poke a small hole in the shell.

Gradually, it chips all the way around the egg.

Finally, the chick forces the egg apart.

Busy parents

Baby birds have enormous appetites, so parents might spend several weeks travelling back and forth from their nests, bringing food for them. Some swallow the food they collect. When they return, they cough it up for the chicks to ea

You might spot a bird flying back to its nest with an insect in its mouth.

The bright insides of these baby song thrushes' mouths show their parents where to drop the food.

First flights

At only a few weeks old, many chicks are strong enough to hop a little way from their nest. By copying their parents and following their own instincts, the chicks learn how to turn their clumsy hops into short flights, and then into longer voyages.

These fluffy robin chicks are strong enough to venture out of their nest, but not yet old enough to fly.

Before trying to take off, a young blue tit practises flapping whilst safely perched.

Taking to the water

Many water bird chicks can swim almost as soon as they hatch out. They usually stay close to an adult at first. If they become cold or tired, they might take a break and let their parent ferry them around on its back.

Mallard ducklings following their mother

Baby grebes hitching a ride from their father

Living together

Some birds keep themselves to themselves, only pairing up once a year to breed. But others eat, sleep and nest in huge groups, living together for long periods of time.

Pecking order

To stop squabbling within a flock, many large groups of birds rank their members according to how aggressive they are. The top birds are the most savage, and they get first choice of food and territory.

...and give loud calls to show how fierce they can be.

Gulls ferociously rip out pieces of grass from the ground...

Cliff colonies

For most of the year, many sea birds live out at sea, swooping over the oceans and bobbing about on the waves. In spring, they come to the shore to find a mate and raise their chicks. They settle on cliff ledges in huge groups called colonies.

There can be thousands of birds in a single cormorant colony.

Two-thirds of the world's gannets nest in groups on cliffs and rocky outcrops in the UK.

Safety in numbers

As winter approaches, the weather grows colder and food becomes scarce. Some birds that live alone during the rest of the year flock together in the winter months to keep warm, find food and watch out for predators.

Long-tailed tits gather in family groups of brothers, sisters, parents and grandparents.

On a snowy lawn in winter, a flock of feeding greenfinches is joined by a hungry sparrow.

Tree sparrow

Team work

Some shore birds hunt in gangs. On muddy beaches, you might see gaggles of geese searching for food or flocks of knots lined up in rows, moving forward together, poking the ground with their beaks as they go.

Brent geese flock together to feed in winter – some search for food, while others act as sentries, keeping a look-out for predators.

Long journeys

Every year, millions of birds migrate vast distances to search for food and places to breed. Some also make these long and dangerous journeys to escape harsh weather conditions.

Fuel for the journey

Some birds travel thousands of miles, making no or very few stops. So that they don't starve on the way, many eat as much as they can for a few weeks before they set out. Others eat on the wing or make frequent feeding stops on the way.

Crossing the globe on their long trips from the Arctic to the Antarctic and back again, Arctic terns only make short stops to eat.

Migrating swallows gobble up flying insects along the way.

Garden warblers can eat enough to double their body weight before they leave, to allow them to cross the Sahara desert non-stop.

During migration, large birds such as white storks, take regular but short snack breaks – they have to watch their weight so they don't become too heavy to fly.

Night flights

Many migrating birds don't make much progress during daylight hours, using this time to rest and eat. They do most of their flying at night, as the air is cooler and the winds are less blustery after dark.

During the day, you might see a flock of migrating birds resting on overhead wires, waiting for nightfall.

Sticking together

Birds often migrate in groups rather than fly solo, as a bird's chances of surviving a predator's attack are greater if it's part of a flock. You might spot migrating birds flying in huge masses or in smaller formations.

When the leader of this flock of whooper swans gets tired, one of the others will take over the lead.

Following the signs

Scientists don't fully understand how birds can navigate over such massive distances, but they have come up with a few theories. Some species might use a combination of these methods.

Shelducks fly in a "V" shape, after a leader.

The position of the Moon and stars may help redwings and other night-fliers to find their way.

Ospreys and other birds that migrate during the day might follow landmarks, such as mountains and islands.

Research on pigeons suggests that they are guided by lines of magnetic forces from the centre of the Earth.

Fast asleep

Like all animals, birds get tired and fall asleep. They don't doze for long though, taking only short naps so they can avoid predators and keep from freezing in cold weather.

Huge groups of starlings roost in trees.

Half awake

Birds can literally sleep with one eye open, and with half of their brain awake, too. This lets them watch for predators whilst also getting some rest. While they sleep, birds don't go limp and floppy, like people do, but stay upright.

Hot spots

Many birds sleep huddled together in groups called roosts, warmed by each other's body heat. Birds that sleep alone look for cosy places to bed down, in tangled undergrowth, or crevices under roofs and in walls.

As a brambling sleeps, its legs stiffen and toes lock around its twiggy perch.

Fulmars fold their legs underneath them to rest on cliff ledges.

On cold nights, you might see wrens squeezing into bushes to roost.

Swifts sleep on the wing, gliding in the air as they doze.

Tucking up

At night, the parts of a bird's body that aren't covered in feathers are particularly vulnerable to the cold. To keep them warm, birds can tuck their beaks into their shoulder feathers or hold one leg up against their bodies.

Waterbirds like these can sleep standing up, with one foot tucked up to their bellies.

Golden plover

Canada goose

This male tufted duck is keeping both its beak and foot warm as it sleeps.

Fluffing out

When it's very cold, you might spot a bird sleeping with its feathers all fluffed up. This traps tiny pockets of air next to its skin. The air is heated by the warmth of the bird's body and stops its body heat escaping.

These feathery mounds are sparrows, sleeping with their feathers raised and beaks tucked in.

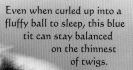

Even when curled up into a fluffy ball to sleep, this blue tit can stay balanced on the thinnest of twigs.

Up at night

As night falls, most birds settle down to sleep but, for a few, dusk is the start of their day. These nocturnal birds spend the daytime dozing, but perk up when the Sun starts to set.

Sharp senses

Nocturnal birds have excellent vision and hearing, which help them to find food in the dark. Even on the gloomiest nights, some owls can see a mouse moving from 2m (6ft) away, and hear it rustling in the grass from an even greater distance.

Of all the European owls, tawny owls can spot their prey in the dimmest light.

Swooping down o its prey, this bar owl is using i super senses to pinpoint th exact position of its target.

Barn owl   Short-eared owl

Owls can twist their heads around and even upside down.

Turning heads

Owls have big eyes to help their night sight. In fact, their eyeballs are so huge that they can hardly move them, so they turn their whole heads instead An owl's neck is very flexible, allowing it to swivel its head in all directions.

Reflecting light

Even birds with smaller eyes can have keen night vision. Nightjars hunt for insects in the evenings, and have shiny layers at the back of their eyeballs to reflect light onto light-sensitive areas of their eyes. This helps them to see their tiny prey in the dim twilight.

Bristles around a nightjar's mouth help it to direct insects into its open beak.

Night calls

Nocturnal birds are often quite difficult to spot but, in the evenings, you can listen out for them calling to each other.

Little owls, like this one, make a mewing sound. Barn owls screech, and long- and short-eared owls hoot. A tawny owl calls out "te-wit", and another answers "te-woo".

Storm petrels purr and cluck around their coastal breeding grounds at night.

Water rails make pig-like squeals and grunts as they skulk about in clumps of reeds at twilight.

Day disguise

Roosting in broad daylight, nocturnal birds are vulnerable to attack from predators. Many have brown and grey feathers, to camouflage them against the trees or forest floors where they sleep.

It's hard to spot a woodcock resting among the dead leaves that carpet its woodland home.

Birdwatching

Birdwatching can be as easy as finding a quiet spot and seeing what birds are around. But a little planning and a few basic pieces of equipment can make it much more fun.

Where to watch

Some birds are most likely to be seen in particular habitats. For example, swans can be found on lakes and rivers, and grouse on moors and mountains. A few birds don't mind people near them, but most are shy, so it's best to watch them quietly, from a place where they can't see you.

You don't have to hide to watch robins, as they are bold near people...

...but less confident birds like these blackcaps may hide or fly off if they sense that a person is close by.

Female

Male

When to watch

Certain times are better than others for birdwatching. You're more likely to spot birds in the morning than in the evening, and in spring and autumn than in summer or winter. But, no matter what time of day or year it is, there's always something to see.

These birds visit Europe in spring.

Chiffchaff

Common tern

Sanderlings are winter visitors to Europe.

It's easier to sketch a bird if it's perched, or standing still on the ground.

Making notes

You could keep a record of the birds you've spotted by making sketches and jotting down when and where you saw them. If you don't recognize a bird, you could make notes about it, then look it up later in a field guide like the one shown at the bottom of this page.

These are the kinds of things that you could note down.

Black head   White collar   8th June
Near canal
Weather – sunny
2:30pm

Dark throat

Sparrow-like body

Perched on tree branch

Bouncing flight pattern

Sketching birds

1. Start with circles for the head and body.

2. Draw lines for the neck, beak, tail and legs.

3. Add details, such as markings or a crest on the head.

Using a field guide

Field guides are books packed with pictures and descriptions of birds, their habitats and behaviour. Some are bulky reference books; others are small enough to slip into a pocket or bag when you go out birdwatching.

With a field guide, you could work out that the bird at the top of this page is a male reed bunting.

SPARROWS, BUNTINGS

HOUSE SPARROW
Very familiar bird. Lives near houses and even in city centres, where it eats scraps. Often seen in flocks. 15cm.

Brown top and female hole age

TREE SPARROW
Usually nests in holes in trees or cliffs. Much less common than house sparrow. 14cm.

YELLOWHAMMER
Found in open country, especially farmland. Feeds on ground. Forms flocks in winter. Sings from the tops of bushes. 17cm.

REED BUNTING
Most common near water, but some nest in dry areas with long grass. May visit bird tables in winter. 15cm.

CORN BUNTING
Nests in cornfields. Sings from posts, bushes or overhead wires. 18cm.

A bird garden

No matter what the season, birds will always visit gardens. You can attract more by providing plenty of places for them to eat, bathe and nest.

Trees and hedges

Leafy branches are not only nesting sites for birds, but also well-stocked larders. Their fruits are an important source of food, especially in autumn, when insects die away.

Berries from Highclere holly bushes keep hungry birds, such as this redwing, fed in the harsh winter months.

The berries that grow on elder trees keep birds fed in winter.

Birds feed on hawthorns' autumn berries and nest and roost in their dense branches.

Thick bramble bushes provide shelter for birds and bear blackberries for them to eat in autumn.

Chaffinch nesting in ivy

Climbing plants

Small birds find shelter in dense climbing plants, such as clematis, ivy and honeysuckle. Honeysuckle is also a source of pollen and nectar, and ivy provides berries in winter.

Honeysuckle

A wild patch

If you leave a corner of a garden to grow wild, you'll soon find plants, such as buttercups, daisies and thistles, springing up. These flowers and grasses attract insects which, in turn, encourage visits from insect-eating birds.

Birds are attracted to the creepy crawlies that feed on these plants.

Shepherd's purse

Creeping buttercup

Goldfinches not only eat the insects on thistles, they feast on thistle's downy seeds, too.

Soft brome

Daisy

Furniture for birds

Putting nest boxes, bird tables and bird baths in a garden keeps birds returning year after year. Place tables or baths in open areas, and nest boxes at least 2m (6½ ft) above the ground, where foxes and cats can't get to them.

Nest boxes come in a variety of designs to suit different birds. This one is for a small species, such as a blue tit.

Birds enjoy fresh water, so clean out your bird bath regularly.

Some birds, such as robins, prefer semi-open nest boxes. These are easier to see inside than closed boxes, like the one above.

Feeding birds

Putting out a wide range of food in a garden will soon attract a variety of birds. You can try leaving seeds, nuts, dry cereal and even grated cheese, in different areas of the garden.

Serving suggestions

Feeding birds can be as simple as leaving seeds on the ground or placing cake crumbs on a branch. You can also put out tables and feeders bought from garden centres and hardware stores.

Larger birds, such as woodpigeons, tend to eat on the ground.

Some smaller birds prefer to eat from bird tables, out of the reach of cats and foxes.

Make a food garland

You will need:

❧ long piece of thread ❧ darning needle
❧ big pieces of popped popcorn

Pull the needle a little way along the folded thread.

1. Make a loop in the middle of the thread and pass it through the hole in the needle.

2. Carefully push the needle through the popcorn, pulling each piece along the thread.

3. Pull the thread out of the needle. Tie knots at both ends. Wind the garland tightly around a branch.

When to feed birds

The most important time to feed birds is in winter when their natural food is scarce, but you can give them a helping hand at any time of the year.

In winter, birds need fatty foods. You can feed them lard or suet by pushing it into the gaps in a pine cone, then hanging it up outside.

Blue tit

Not wanting to wait their turn, these tits are fighting and flapping over a bird feeder.

Great tit

Make a bird cake

You will need:

🌰 nuts 🌰 cake crumbs 🌰 oatmeal
🌰 dried fruit 🌰 250g (0.5lb) solid fat

Stir with a wooden spoon.

1. Mix about 500g (1lb) of all the dry ingredients in a heat-resistant bowl.

2. In a saucepan, melt the fat over a low heat. Carefully pour it over the mixture. Leave it to set.

3. When the cake is cold, turn it out. Put it outside on a raised platform, such as a bird table.

Bird detective

Sometimes you might not see all the birds that live nearby, but you can keep an eye out for clues that tell you where they've been and even what they've been eating.

Finding feathers

In summer, many birds grow new feathers to replace their old, worn ones. You can find discarded feathers in spots where birds roost or eat. Make sure you wash your hands after touching them.

Curlew feather

To identify the feathers you find, you can try to match them with the colours and markings of birds in a field guide.

Pheasant feather

Mallard feather

Magpie feather

Barn owl feather

Jay feather

Footprints with one long toe behind three front toes belong to birds that perch.

Tracking footprints

A bird's footprints are often hard to spot, as birds don't spend much time on the ground and, when there, they tread lightly. If you find a bird's tracks, look for clues to where it lives and how it moves. Hopping birds have paired tracks, while walking birds' prints lie one in front of the other.

A wading bird's tracks show long, spreading toes.

Many birds that swim have webbed prints.

Ducks leave webbed tracks on muddy banks.

Bird pellets

Some birds swallow their food whole, then cough up pellets of the parts they can't digest. These parcels can be made up of fur, bones, feathers or insect parts. If you come across a pellet, you can look what's inside.

Gulls forage on rubbish dumps so, as well as bits of food, there might be some other odds and ends in their pellets.

Fish bone

Scrap of foil

Looking inside a pellet

Water with a few drops of disinfectant

Wash your hands when you've finished.

1. Soak the pellet for an hour. Put it on an old newspaper. Use cocktail sticks to prise it apart.

2. Using a pair of tweezers, pick out the hard parts, such as teeth and bones.

3. Clean the hard bits with a dry paint brush and look at them with a magnifying glass.

Signs of feeding

You can find out what food the birds in your area eat by looking for signs of pecking on nuts, cones, fruits and plants.

Like this fieldfare, many birds can't finish a big piece of food in one go, and will often leave it half-eaten.

Birds leave peck marks in nuts.

Other animals, such as rodents, might leave teeth marks.

Town and city birds

Birds live in all kinds of places, even those built specifically for people. In towns and cities all over the world, you'll find birds thriving amidst the buildings, bustle and traffic.

Tame birds

It's easy to watch birds that live in town and city centres, as they're not difficult to find and are used to being around people. They're often reasonably tame, but it's safest not to touch them.

Unruffled by passing traffic and pedestrians, a feral pigeon takes a refreshing drink from a public fountain.

Pigeons often fly over built-up areas in huge groups.

Soaring over busy streets, gulls scout for food scraps.

Noisy flocks of chattering starlings gather on rooftops.

City visitors

Some country birds visit urban regions every winter, to take advantage of the food and warmth that built-up areas provide.

In winter, skylarks fly from the open countryside to city parks and wasteground.

City songs

The noise of the city can often drown out birds' songs. To make themselves heard, some city birds sing at a higher pitch than their country cousins. You can also hear some birds singing at night.

City great tits sing higher melodies than country great tits.

As night falls, street lights turn on, prompting robins to burst into song.

On your doorstep

For birds that live near people's homes, finding food can be as simple as turning up on their human neighbours' doorsteps.

Blue tits occasionally peck holes in milk bottle tops to sip the milk inside.

The radiators of parked cars make good feeding grounds for insect-eating house sparrows.

White storks sometimes construct their huge nests in chimneys.

Building sites

Some of the best places to see urban birds' nests are in parks and on wasteground. Look out for them nestled in trees and bushes, or sitting by ponds and lakes. You might spot them in more built-up areas, too.

Undisturbed junkyards and dumping grounds are full of nooks and crannies where city birds, like this robin, can build their nests.

In the country

From grassy fields to boggy marshes, the countryside offers a wide range of habitats for birds. You'll spot different kinds of birds in each area.

Woods and forests

Places where there are a lot of trees make good nesting sites for birds. A tree's fruits, nuts, seeds and even their insect inhabitants also provide birds with an array of tasty treats.

Hungry crossbills find seeds by prising open cones that grow on pine trees.

Jays collect acorns from oak trees, bury them, then dig them up later when they need food.

If you find a hole surrounded by mud in a tree, it may be a nuthatch's nesting hole.

Treecreepers crawl up tree trunks, devouring insects.

Fields and hedges

Hedgerows, fields and meadows are stocked full of food for birds. They feast on plants and small animals in hedges and amongst crops, and gobble up insects that buzz around farm animals, too.

Pheasants nest and feed in fields.

Heathland birds

In summer, it may seem as if heaths are only inhabited by plant life, but they're also teeming with insects, so attract many insect-eating birds. As there aren't many trees around, birds tend to nest in or under bushes.

Stonechats and linnets nest in thick gorse bushes on heaths.

Stonechat

Linnets

Boggy marshes

Marshes are open areas of grass and reeds, which are wet for most of the time. Many marsh birds live close to the ground, so are difficult to spot, but you might see some small birds perched on top of the rustling reeds.

Reed warblers sometimes rest on reedtops, but prefer to stay hidden further down.

Ponds and streams

Still or slow-flowing water attracts lots of different types of birds. Some spend most of their lives in and around the water, while others just visit to have a drink or take a dip.

Kingfishers grab fish from the water, then fly to a perch with the fish in their beaks.

This tufted duck is "upending" to grab prey beneath the surface.

Tufted duck right way up

A shoveler duck sieves food from the water with its bill.

Moorhens spend as much time on land as they do in the water.

Seashore birds

A trip to the seaside will give you plenty of opportunities to spot birds. Watch out for them feeding on sea-soaked shores or nesting on dizzying clifftops or grassy sandhills.

Sea and sand

At the water's edge, you can look for birds hunting for little creatures in the sand, or circling in the sky, waiting to grab leftovers from picnickers.

Further inland, low, sandy hills called dunes are home to a range of plants and insects. These attract birds, who come to the dunes to feed or set up home.

In sand dunes, shelducks make their nests in old rabbit holes.

Sanderlings run back and forth across the sand, on the look-out for worms and shellfish.

From the air, herring gulls drop shells onto the rocks below to open them.

Stony beaches

The rocks and pebbles on a beach can be very useful to birds. They camouflage their eggs, are places to find tasty seaside animals, and are handy for breaking open shells.

Oystercatchers prise limpets from rocks with their beaks.

Muddy shores

Where rivers meet the sea, birds gather on the salty mudflats that are exposed at low tide. In autumn and winter, you can see migrating birds feeding and resting here before and after their long journeys.

In winter, knots and bar-tailed godwits fly to British saltmarshes from their Arctic breeding grounds.

Bar-tailed godwit

Knot

Wading birds like these use their long beaks to probe for food in the soft ground.

You can see redshanks on muddy shores all year round.

Curlew

Avocet

Dunlin

Craggy cliffs

In spring, lots of birds that have spent the winter out at sea, come ashore to make nests on cliffs. You might spot a cliff covered by a huge colony of just one type of bird, or spy a mixture of different birds perched on its ledges.

Puffins make burrows in grassy cliffsides to lay eggs inside.

Although all these birds lay their eggs on cliffs, each one uses different materials to construct its nest.

Gannets scour the beach for seaweed to use as building material.

Instead of making nests, razorbills lay their eggs in crevices.

This shag has built a twiggy nest for its chicks.

Harsh environments

High up on bleak moors and misty mountains, there's very little food or shelter for birds. Some of the world's toughest birds live in these challenging habitats.

High and low

Barren landscapes are good places to look for birds of prey. In mountains, they soar high on strong winds and nest on towering, rocky ledges. On moors, they stay close to the ground, nesting in heather and bracken, and flying low to look for small animals to eat.

Golden eagles prey on hares and other small mountain mammals.

Short-eared owls hunt on moors during the day.

Perching motionless, a merlin looks out over the moors, watching for prey.

Hen harriers nest amongst moorland plants.

Short-toed eagles snap up snakes that slither through long, moorland grass.

Hidden away

Moors and mountains are home to some types of game birds, which are hunted by birds of prey and by people, too. With so many enemies, game birds have to be masters of disguise, spending a lot of time crouched in bushes and thick patches of undergrowth.

Ptarmigans nest hidden among rocks or bushes.

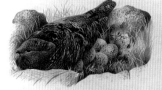

To help it hide in all seasons, a willow grouse's feathers change from brown in summer to white in winter.

Unfussy eaters

As there isn't much food in their moorland habitats, ravens eat almost anything. They mainly feed on dead animals, even pecking out the eyeballs. If there aren't any animals or insects around, they'll resort to eating grass.

Ravens tear meat with their strong, hooked beaks.

Going for a dip

Rivers and streams that run down mountains usually flow very rapidly. Most birds don't go near these fierce waters, but you might spot a few small birds dipping their beaks in from a safe perching place.

Dippers swim, dive, and walk along the bottom of fast-flowing streams in search of food.

Grey wagtails stand on rocks to snatch water insects from rapids.

Birds in danger

Over the years, many birds have been harmed by people, both accidentally and deliberately. Today, there are laws to protect birds, but they still have man-made dangers to face.

Altering habitats

When habitats, such as fields or woods, are farmed intensively or cleared for construction, birds can find themselves homeless. Those that can't adapt to living in other areas begin to die out.

The number of black tailed godwits declin when their wetland breeding grounds are drained for farming.

This photograph may be the closest you'll come to a tree sparrow. This species has been dying out, as an increasing use of pesticides has made it harder for them to find insects to eat.

Corn buntings die out when the weeds they feed on are removed to make space for crops.

Dangerous waters

Rubbish, waste chemicals and oi are sometimes spilled or even illega dumped on beaches and into rivers and oceans, harming water birds.

Plastic rings that used to hold cans together can strangle birds.

It's helpful to cut up the rings, and put them in a recycling bin.

Toxic chemicals

For birds of prey, there's a risk that the animals they eat could have fed on plants sprayed with various chemical pesticides and weed killers. These chemicals can build up in the bird's body and poison it.

In the 1950s and 60s, hundreds of peregrine falcons perished when a pesticide called DDT was sprayed on crops. DDT is now banned.

Red kites are harmed by feeding on rodents that have been poisoned as pests.

Hunting

Some local populations of game birds have been hunted to alarmingly low levels. Many countries now have restrictions on the number of birds that can be shot for sport.

Red-legged partridge

In some European countries, legal and illegal hunting has drastically reduced the red-legged partridge and capercaillie populations.

Capercaillie

Trapping and collecting

Trappers catch wild songbirds illegally and sell them as pets. Collectors also steal birds' eggs. The rarer the bird, the more its eggs are sought after.

Trappers target songbirds, such as linnets, to be sold as cage birds.

Protecting birds

Many organizations look after birds, giving them safe places
feed and nest. You can help birds by joining a bird protectio
group or simply by caring for the birds in your area.

Managing the land

If a bird species is dying out, conservation
organizations work with landowners,
advising them on how to manage their
land in ways that will help these
threatened birds.

Farmers are helped to make
wet meadows on their la
providing feeding and
nesting sites for bird
such as lapwings.

Protected places

Some governments, charities and
private landowners have set aside lar
for wildlife to live on, where building
and hunting is very tightly restricted.
These nature reserves can range from
a few fields to vast national parks.

Stretches of water on nature reserves can
attract many varieties of ducks, geese and
other freshwater birds.

You might
spot a colourful
kingfisher, like this
one, perched beside a
quiet backwater on
a nature reserve.

Shelduck

Goldeneye

Brent goose

Finding a nest

Discovering a bird's nest can be very exciting, but it's important not to touch it. If a bird senses that its nest has been disturbed, it may abandon it as well as any eggs inside it.

In many countries, it's illegal to move a nest, even if it's on the side of a house, like this house martin's nest.

Although this song thrush's nest is empty, the bird could return to it when it's ready to lay eggs again.

Finding baby birds

A chick sitting on the ground by itself may look as if it needs rescuing, but its parents are likely to be close by, watching over it. If a chick has fallen out of its nest and can't get back, you can look for the nest nearby and gently put it inside.

Blackbird chick

Young robin

Young lapwing

A featherless chick on the ground is likely to have fallen out of its nest.

Young birds covered in down feathers are probably old enough to look after themselves.

Safe haven

Gardens are often the main source of food for local birds but, even here, they might face dangers. People can make gardens safe for birds by keeping them free from chemical pest killers and by putting quick-release bell collars on their cats, so birds can hear them coming.

Myths and legends

In ancient times, birds were seen as symbols of power and religious figures. Today, birds still play an important role in the culture and religion of people all over the world.

Power and glory

Throughout history, the leaders of nations have used birds as symbols of authority and freedom. Today, birds still appear on many flags and coats of arms.

The bird of paradise is the national emblem of Papua New Guinea and it features on the country's flag.

Roman soldiers were led into battle by a standard-bearer, whose job it was to hold up a statue of an eagle.

Curious creatures

Many ancient cultures have legends of mythical birds with magical abilities. One such bird is the phoenix, which dies in a burst of flames, only to be reborn, as a new phoenix rises from the ashes

Phoenixes appear in legends from Egypt, Greece and China. The stories vary, but many describe the bird as having flaming wing and a tail of fire.

Sacred symbols

Stories from many religions link birds with higher powers, such as gods or goddesses. Birds were seen as suitable symbols due to their grace and strength but, most of all, because of their superhuman ability to fly.

Hundreds of years ago, the Aztec peoples of Central America regarded quetzal birds as symbols of their god of the air and sky.

In the Bible, the story of Jesus's baptism tells of God's spirit coming down to him in the form of a dove.

The Ancient Greeks believed that Athena, their goddess of wisdom, could turn herself into an owl.

Soul carriers

Many legends tell of birds carrying people's souls. There are tales of sea birds delivering the souls of dead sailors to heaven, of doves taking lovers' souls to their sweethearts, and even of souls looking like birds with human heads.

It was considered bad luck to kill these sea birds, as people thought they carried the souls of drowned sailors.

Albatross

Black-headed gull

Ancient Egyptians believed they had bird-like souls which flew from their bodies when they died.

Fascinating facts

Biggest...

Ostriches are both the tallest and the heaviest birds. They reach a height of up to 2.5m (8ft) tall and a weight of 156.5kg (350lbs).

Despite being the heaviest birds, ostriches are also the fastest runners, reaching speeds of up to 97kph (60mph).

...and smallest

The tiniest birds are bee hummingbirds. They're even smaller than bumblebees and weigh just 1.6g (0.06oz).

Widest wingspan

When fully stretched, the wings of a wandering albatross measure about 3.5m (11½ft) from tip to tip, the same as two men lying end to end.

Wandering albatross

Chatterboxes

African grey parrots can be taught to say around 800 words. They can learn to recite short poems, and even sing lyrics.

As well as words, African grey parrots can mimic other noises, such as ringing doorbells and pinging microwaves.

Bumper beaks

Australian pelicans have the longest beaks. They can grow up to 45cm (18in) long, which is about the length of a computer keyboard.

Most feathers

Tundra swans (also called North American whistling swans) are covered with over 25,000 feathers.

Frequent flappers

Hummingbirds usually flap their wings 40-80 times a second. When a male is trying to impress a female, it increases its flapping to 200 times a second.

A ruby-throated hummingbird flaps about 80 times a second as it hovers.

Breathtaking divers

Emperor penguins can stay under water for longer than any other bird, diving for up to 18 minutes in one breath.

Emperor penguins

Fast movers

The speediest swimmers are gentoo penguins. They can zip along at speeds of up to 27kph (17mph).

Its torpedo-shaped body helps this gentoo penguin reach its top speeds when swimming under water.

Treetop mansions

Bald eagles build nests that are around 3m (9½ft) wide and 6m (20ft) deep. That's big enough to fit several people inside.

Counting chickens

Of the 100,000 million birds in the world, around 3,000 million are domestic chickens.

INDEX

ACKNOWLEDGEMENTS

Cover design: Joanne Kirkby

Additional designs: Reuben Barrance

Artwork co-ordinator: Louise Breen

PHOTO CREDITS (t = top, m = middle, b = bottom, l = left, r = right)
1 © Warren Photographic; 2 © Doug Houghton/Alamy; 4-5 © David Tipling/Alamy;
7b © www.ianbutlerphotography.co.uk; 9b © Nature Picture Library/Alamy; 10br © Nikki
Edmunds/Alamy; 12-13 © Ken Plows Wildlife Photography; 15b © Andrew Darrington /
Alamy; 16bl © Specialpictures.nl/Alamy; 19m © Mike Wilkes/naturepl.com; 20mr © Warren
Photographic; 22b © Robert Harding Picture Library Ltd/Alamy; 26m © birdpix/Alamy; 29b
© Gerry Ellis/GLOBIO/Science Faction/Getty Images; 31t © John Daniels/ardea.com; 33m ©
blickwinkel/Alamy; 35m © Malcolm Schuyl/Alamy; 37b © Arco Images/Alamy; 38mr © Digital
Zoo/Digital Vision/Getty Images; 42m © Brian Mcgeough/Alamy; 45m © Warren Photographic;
47b © David Kjaer/naturepl.com; 48b © Altrendo images/Getty Images; 52m © imagebroker/
Alamy; 54b © David Osborn/Alamy; 56bl © Steven Round Photography; 58br © Richard Ford/
Natural Visions; 60b © MARY EVANS/BRENDA HARTILL; 63b © Gistimages/Alamy

ILLUSTRATORS Dave Ashby, Mike Atkinson, Graham Austin, John Barber, Andrew
Becket, Joyce Bee, Isabel Bowring, Trevor Boyer, Hilary Burn, Kuo Kang Chen, Brin Edwards,
Sandra Fernandez, Denise Finney, Wayne Forde, Don Forrest, Toby Gibson, Alan Harris,
Christine Howes, Roy Hutchinson, Ian Jackson, Elaine Keenan, Roger Kent, Aziz Khan, Colin
King, Steven Kirk, Ken Lilly, Stephen Lings, Mick Loates, Rachel Lockwood, Kevin Lyles,
Joseph McEwan, Ian McNee, Andy Martin, David Mead, Richard Millington, Annabel Milne,
Dee Morgan, Robert Morton, Richard Orr, Charles Pearson, Julie Piper, Gillian Platt, Maurice
Pledger, David Quinn, Chris Shields, John Sibbick, Peter Stebbing, Elena Temporin, John
Thompson-Steinkrauss, Ian Wallace, John Woodcock, David Wright, Phil Weare, John Yates